A Lover's Dismantling: Fragments of a Scenic Discourse

by Elena Guiochins

Translated from the Spanish by Andy Bragen

NoPassport Press Dreaming the Americas Series

A Lover's Dismantling

By Elena Guiochins, translation by Andy Bragen

Copyright 2012. Volume copyright 2016. Individual copyright is retained by original authors and translators.

All rights reserved. Except for brief passages quoted in newspaper, magazine, radio, or television reviews, no part of this book may be reproduced in any form or by any means, electronic or mechanical, without permission in writing from the author. Professionals and amateurs are hereby warned that this material, being fully protected under the Copyright Laws of the United States of America and of all the other countries of the Berne and Universal Copyright Conventions, is subject to royalty. All rights including, but not limited to professional, amateur, recording, motion picture, recitation, lecturing, public reading, radio and television broadcasting, and the rights of translation into foreign languages are expressly reserved. Particular emphasis is placed on the question of readings and all uses of this play by educational institutions, permission for which must be secured from the author. For all rights, including amateur and stock performances, contact respective authors' representatives. Contact for Translator: Andy Bragen, abragen@gmail.com

NoPassport Press Dreaming the Americas Series

NoPassport Press, PO Box 1786, South Gate, CA 90280 USA; e-mail: NoPassportPress@aol.com, website: www.nopassport.org

Cover photo: courtesy of Conjuro Teatro, Mexico.

ISBN: 978-1-365-23068-4

A Lover's Dismantling:
Fragments of a Scenic Discourse

By Elena Guiochins

was translated by Andy Bragen with a commission from the Lark Play Development Center's Mexico/United States Playwright Exchange program.

This print edition of the translation is a collaboration between the Lark and NoPassport theatre alliance and press.

NoPassport: NoPassport is a theatre alliance & press devoted to live, virtual and print action, advocacy and change toward the fostering of cross-cultural and aesthetic diversity in the arts with an emphasis on human and environmental rights theatre actions. NoPassport Press' Dreaming the Americas Series and Theatre & Performance PlayTexts Series promotes new writing for the stage, texts on theory and practice and theatrical translations. www.nopassport.org

Series Editors: Randy Gener, Jorge Huerta, Mead K. Hunter, Otis Ramsey-Zoe, Stephen Squibb, Caridad Svich (founding editor)

Advisory Board: Daniel Banks, Amparo Garcia-Crow, Maria M. Delgado, Randy Gener, Elana Greenfield, Christina Marin, Antonio Ocampo Guzman, Sarah Cameron Sunde, Saviana Stanescu, Tamara Underiner, Patricia Ybarra

NoPassport is supported entirely through private donations, and is under the fiscal sponsorship of Fractured Atlas. To contribute online: https://www.fracturedatlas.org/site/fiscal/profile?id=2623

The Lark's Mexico/United States Playwright Exchange

The Lark is an international theater laboratory based in New York City that is devoted to supporting playwrights and stories that reflect the vibrancy of our community. At the center of The Lark's mission is our faith in playwrights whose work tranforms us beyond our own experience and the belief that global exchange expands our humanity.

While The Lark's work with Mexican artists started in 2000, The México Playwright Exchange, as a formal reciprocal program, began in 2006 as one The Lark's Global Exchange initiatives. The program's core activity is a residency that brings Mexican writers to the U.S. and U.S. writers to México to work on translations of their work. The program is designed to create stage-worthy translations of plays that can subsequently be produced, published, and taught. The vision is to establish ongoing channels of artistic collaboration and communication between Mexican and U.S. theater artists and their respective communities. Andrea Thome is the México/United States Playwright Exchange Program Director. In 2016, the program celebrated its first ten years.

The México/U.S. Playwright Exchange Program is a collaboration between The Lark and Fondo Nacional para la Cultura y las Artes (México's National Fund for Culture and Arts). The program has had additional support from the Robert Sterling Clark Foundation, New York City Department of Cultural Affairs in partnership with the City Council and The Mexican Cultural Institute of New York.

The Lark is led by Artistic Director John Clinton Eisner and Managing Director Michael Robertson. For more information on the initiatives, artists and plays of The Lark visit www.larktheatre.org For an archive of the translated scripts of the México/United States Playwright Exchange visit:
http://www.larktheatre.org/what-we-do/our-initiatives/mexico-united-states-translation-exchange/script-mexicounited-states-playwright-exchange/

A Lover's Dismantling: Fragments of a Scenic Discourse
by Elena Guiochins, translated by Andy Bragen

"There are only two kinds of thoughts: memories and imagination. This story of two couples finding, living, and losing love wanders whimsically through time, distance, dreams, and heartbreak."

A Lover's Dismantling:

Fragments of a Scenic Discourse

Elena Guiochins (Writer) Member of the National System of Arts Creators since 2010. Dramatist, stage director, translator and teacher. She has participated in national and international festivals such as the Mousson d`eté y the Neue Dramatik Schaubühne. Fellow FONCA and artistic residency programs at The Banff Centre, Canadá, Writers Room and Lark Play Development Program in N.Y. and Centre des Auteurs Dramatics in Montréal, Québec. Her most recent play, *Translucid@* directed by herself in 2016, was produced by the Coordination of Theater's National Institute of Fine Arts.

Andy Bragen (Translator) Andy's plays and translations have been seen and heard at numerous theatres, including PS122, Brown/Trinity Playwrights Rep, and Soho Rep. His play *This is My Office* premiered off-Broadway with The Play Company in the autumn of 2013. He has an MFA from Brown University and is a member of New Dramatists. For more information: www.andybragen.com

A Lover's Dismantling:
Fragments of a Scenic Discourse

**Credits for the Halcyon Theatre
Alcyone Theatre Festival in Chicago, 2012.**

A Lover's Dismantling
Jin Kim (Jin)
Alexis Schaetzle (Alexis)
Riso Straley (Riso)
Laura Stephenson (Laura)

Alex Gualino (Director)

Tony Adams (Artistic Director, Halcyon Theatre)
www.halcyontheatre.org

"A Lover's Dismantling" was written between October 2008 and February 2009, during a rehearsal workshop with the Mexico City based theatrical troupe Conjuro Teatro. The characters at that time were given the first names of the actors who developed the piece. In this version, the character names listed are the first names of the actors involved with the 2009 Mexico/United States Playwright Exchange at the Lark Play Development Center, where the translation received a workshop. The names should be changed to match those of the actors in future workshops and productions.

Performers in original Mexico City Production:
Carolina Contreras
Alejandra Marín
Héctor Hugo Peña
Julio Escartín

Performers in Lark Workshop:
Crystal Finn
Annie Henk
Armando Riesco
Gerry Rodriguez

Do we mean love when we say love?
-Samuel Beckett

1. IN TRANSIT

An airport. Two men in the boarding area. Each one drags a rolling suitcase. They sit down beside each other.

GERRY: "There are only two kinds of thoughts: memories and imagination". That's the phrase than ran through Armando's mind, like a kind of mantra, whenever he was about to board a plane.

ARMANDO: I was alone. It was night. The flight was running over three hours late. But what are three hours on eternity's clock? Gerry was the first to break the silence.

GERRY: Looks interesting...

ARMANDO: ...

GERRY: The book.

ARMANDO: It's not a book.

GERRY: ...

ARMANDO: Characters and events shape our life stories. Whenever my thoughts return to that precise moment, that night in Jakarta airport, I picture that man who wouldn't stop asking me questions. I think about everything around me, and try to understand my life's meaning, its specific events. Like a wounded dog, I have sniffed out tracks of my existence disguised as coincidences; they have shown me the power, the will of destiny...

GERRY *(referring to Armando's suitcase)*: Heavy, right?

ARMANDO: Huh?

GERRY: Excess baggage...

ARMANDO: ...

GERRY: Suddenly it came to me. Our context determines how we interpret everything that follows. For me, it all goes back to the beginning.

2. POSTCARDS FROM OUR STORY

Armando and Annie are seated in front of a judge: Gerry. Nearby, Crystal, the lawyer.

JUDGE: Name of wife: Mrs. Annie Small, will not keep her husband's name, will retake her maiden name: Castle. Husband and Wife reside separately, have since November 7, 2007, Mr. Small having moved out as was stipulated in the interim agreement. Forfeiture of matrimonial rights. Husband and Wife own no real estate in common.

Ms. Castle retains the rented apartment. Mr. and Mrs. Small executed the division of furniture as specified in the addendum to the interim agreement. Husband and Wife acknowledge having taken possession of all clothing, objects, and jewelry belonging to them personally, or belonging to their respective families. The parties do not share any bank accounts or common lines of credit. With respect to children: The Husband and Wife have one son. Amado Small Castle was born on September 23, 2001 in Mexico City. Husband and Wife choose to share joint legal custody. Both parents shall retain full parental rights and responsibilities. Both parents shall confer with one another so that major decisions affecting the best interests and welfare of the child may be determined jointly, where reasonably possible. We further agree that Mrs. Annie Small will have sole physical custody of the child. The parties agree to share in an equitable fashion the child's birthday, holidays and all vacations. Furthermore, the parties agree to allow the other parent to have a frequent and liberal visitation with the child. The non-custodial parent will have the right to be with the child at least, but not limited to, as follows: the first, third and fifth weekend of each month from Thursday afternoon, and Friday afterschool, until Sunday evening at 7. The Father will pick the Child up from, and return him to, the Mother's residence. During the first half of school vacations in even years and the second half of the same vacations in odd years, the child will reside with the Father. Mr. Small will pay a monthly sum of eight thousand pesos for the support and education of his son. With regard to alimony, the Husband and Wife declare that no disparity exists between their incomes and thus it is not necessary. Conforming to the regulations of article 265 of the civil code, Mr. and Mrs. Small are cancelling the payments that they have mutually contributed to their life insurance policies, and likewise any other contribution stipulated throughout the length of the marriage under any form. The costs of the divorce will be equally shared, as will the legal fees. *(To Crystal)* Do you have anything to add, Counsel?

CRYSTAL: No, Your Honor, you'll need to check with my clients.

JUDGE: Madam, is this acceptable to you?

ANNIE: Yes, Your Honor.

JUDGE: Mr. Small?

ARMANDO: Yes?

JUDGE: Is this acceptable to you?

ARMANDO: Yes, yes, it's fine. Everything's fine.

JUDGE: I then certify this divorce on this day, the 20th of March 2009. Sign here please. Madam....Sir...If you please, initial the first three sheets.

Annie and Armando sign in silence.

3. FRAGMENTS OF A DISCOURSE

GERRY: I saw her first. That night in Jakarta airport, you were wearing your flight attendant's uniform. You crossed the room rapidly while I tried to speak with that double of mine from the future who misunderstood the meaning of my words. His interpretations became his experience, not mine. I saw you first.

GERRY: Are you travelling alone?

ARMANDO: No.

Armando opens a suitcase from which a woman emerges.

ARMANDO: I'm travelling with my wife.

ANNIE *(extending her hand to Gerry)*: Annie. Nice to meet you.

GERRY: Gerry...

ANNIE: Are you travelling alone?

ARMANDO: Gerry thinks that the meal he had on the previous flight must have disagreed with him even though he can't remember what exactly he ate, possibly shrimp, it always does him in. What did the flight attendant offer him while they were crossing the sky? Chicken or pasta? And that woman who just asked the question: did she actually come out of the suitcase?

GERRY: If a surgeon were to enter my brain right now, he'd end up lost and famished, and he'd have no idea what I ate today.

A flight attendant offers dinner.

CRYSTAL: Chicken or pasta?

ARMANDO: Pasta.

ANNIE: The same.

CRYSTAL: Chicken or pasta?

GERRY: I don't know...

CRYSTAL: There are no wrong answers....Chicken!

3.1 FRAGMENT/AFTER DINNER

Annie and Armando finish clearing the dinner plates

ANNIE: They look like they're very much in love.

ARMANDO: They won't last.

ANNIE: It seems to me like they adore each other.

ARMANDO: She's very young, too young.

ANNIE: The age difference isn't necessarily an obstacle, at least not between them. Crystal strikes me as very intelligent and mature.

ARMANDO: All she ended up doing was showing off her own ignorance.

ANNIE: You're very harsh, did you know that?

ARMANDO: My brother specializes in shallowness. This too will pass soon, no doubt.

ANNIE: I saw him as too in love.

ARMANDO: That expression seems so absurd to me: "Too in love". Who ever heard of anything that was "too beautiful"? Too in love is a banal notion.

ANNIE: Are you going to open the other bottle?

ARMANDO: You don't think it's "too much"?

ANNIE: I think that your notion of love is banal. Too much so.

Time change.

3.2 FRAGMENT/AFTER-DINNER CHAT

GERRY: Everything was delicious. *(To Annie)* You're a mar-vel-ous chef.

CRYSTAL: Pour me some more wine?

ANNIE: How long have you two been together?

CRYSTAL: Hard to say. We haven't been counting time.

ARMANDO: For someone so young, you seem to have seen it all.

GERRY: My brother is obsessed with time. He fixes clocks, did I mention that?

ANNIE: Armando and I have been together for ten years.

ARMANDO: An eternity.

CRYSTAL: I don't worry so much about time.

ARMANDO: 'Cause you're a baby, that's why.

CRYSTAL: Do you have any children?

ANNIE: One. Amado, he's six.

CRYSTAL: Amado, the Beloved. What a beautiful name.

ANNIE: How did you and Gerry meet?

CRYSTAL: On a speed date.

ANNIE: A speed date?

CRYSTAL: They're high-speed singles events.

GERRY: A system of quick dates among groups formed through consideration of member profiles and, in some cases, religious orientations.

ARMANDO: And you guys were in which category: God is optional?

ANNIE: Now I remember, a friend of mine told me about these kinds of gatherings a while ago.

CRYSTAL: For someone who travels as much as I do, it's a good way to meet people.

GERRY: Crystal is a flight attendant.

ARMANDO: So thanks to this metaphysical casting call you met the man of your life in seven minutes?

ANNIE: Does anyone want more dessert?

They all shake their heads no.

ANNIE: Are you sure? Well, I do.

GERRY: The first time I saw Crystal was in the airport.

ARMANDO: You may have mixed her up with another flight attendant from the same airline – in their uniforms they're all the same.

GERRY: No way. *(To Crystal)* It was you. *(To Annie)* That dress really suits you.

CRYSTAL: Yeah, you look super cute.

ANNIE: I haven't worn it in a while. So, I'm still not clear: Did you meet in the airport, or on a speed date?

CRYSTAL: Through friends...

GERRY: Whom we met on a speed date.

CRYSTAL: Exactly.

GERRY: First, I saw her in the airport, and then one year later these friends introduced us.

ARMANDO: How does it feel to spend so much time up in the air?

ANNIE: You must travel a lot.

CRYSTAL: Yes, all the time. But that's what I like about it.

ARMANDO *(to Gerry):* She's not right for you. I know these sorts of women. When they're up in the air they're one thing, and when their feet land on the ground, they're something altogether different.

CRYSTAL: I don't seem to be making a very good impression on your brother.

GERRY: Nothing makes a good impression on Armando, and when he's got wine in him, it's even worse.

ANNIE: It's not hard for you two?

CRYSTAL/GERRY: What?

ANNIE: To spend so much time apart?

CRYSTAL: No, it's fine.

ARMANDO: How old is this girl?

ANNIE: Why are you so concerned with her age?

ARMANDO: He's my brother, I don't want to see him hurt.

GERRY: I'm happy. What are you talking about?

ANNIE *(to Armando):* You're acting like an idiot.

ARMANDO: We're among family, no?

ANNIE: Anyone want more wine?

CRYSTAL: Yes, thanks.

GERRY: My brother is the ultimate contrarian.

ARMANDO: Like I said, I don't want to see you hurt.

GERRY: One drinks however one can from one's own cup. I drink mine, and you yours. Cheers!

ARMANDO: Nonsense. Shallow minds slop from the same trough. Cheers!

ANNIE: Hunger is desire. Where there is nothing, I beg for something. Cheers!

CRYSTAL: A hungry person is a creature on the hunt. I'm always starving. *(To Armando)* I'm twenty.

ARMANDO: Who are they trying to kid?

ANNIE *(to Armando):* Don't you think you've had enough?

ARMANDO: I already have a long enough list of things I'm expected to hide. Who cares!?

GERRY *(to Crystal):* You're going already?

CRYSTAL: Yes, it's getting pretty late. I'm supposed to drop by Taquito's place.

GERRY: Do you want me to come with you?

CRYSTAL: It's just going to be techno music and a bunch of kids dancing. I don't think you'd have much fun. I'll call you once I'm there.

GERRY: All right. Enjoy yourself.

Crystal says goodbye and leaves.

ANNIE: She's adorable.

GERRY: Yes, she is.

ARMANDO: She's a lost teenager!

GERRY: Once again my brother has made a snap decision about my destiny.

ANNIE *(to Armando):* The disproportion of your comments is irritating. Really Armando...

ARMANDO: What do you want: To devote my life to the greater good, I'd have to go through some real shit first.

GERRY: Love doesn't need to be suffocating.

ARMANDO: Now you sound like your gay friends.

GERRY: What has come into my life is beauty. Period.

ARMANDO: I'll just add that to your list of gay sayings.

ANNIE: Okay, that's enough.

Annie put on some music. SOMETHING by the Beatles.

ANNIE: Who wants to dance with me?

Armando pours himself another drink. Gerry and Annie dance.

4. ARMANDO

Armando sings SOMETHING by the Beatles.

ARMANDO: I was born in a house where romantic love didn't exist, on the contrary, any reference to it was promptly ignored. The dictatorship of the feminine: a house of women, of solitary women. My widowed grandmother, eternally grief-stricken by my grandfather's abandonment. My mother (apparently alone), full of mysteries when it came to what she referred to as the sentimental terrain. Her relationship with my father, blurred by the passage of time, was always kept in the greatest obscurity for me. Later I would discover that the true sentimental terrain of my mother wasn't beside a man.

GERRY: I met her at a speed dating event. Mexico City. Saturday afternoon. Present day.

5. SENTIMENTAL SITUATION.

Two couples seated face to face at cafe tables. The sound of a bell starts the dialogue for each couple, and will also indicate its completion, the changing of partners at the adjacent table emulating the standard dynamic of a speed date. Each one of the actors has a nametag pasted on his/her chest.

CRYSTAL: Your family is dysfunctional too…we have so much in common. Can you believe it? And what do you do?

ARMANDO: I sing in a bar. And I fix clocks.

GERRY: I'm feeling something here. *(gesturing to his stomach)* It happens whenever I'm nervous. I'm feeling little sharp pains. No, it's not what you're thinking, it's not an ulcer. Truth is I'm very healthy.

ANNIE: I'm the middle child, and I'm the only one who entered the world via natural birth. My sister arrived with forceps, and thanks to that she's always so tense, the poor thing ...my brother via caesarean, I came straight out the chute - animal-style!

GERRY: What's most important to me in a woman is that she be pretty and sincere...above all pretty....

CRYSTAL: ...Generosity, having confidence in the other, communication, playfulness, smiles, learning together how to listen, mutual respect, neither hoping nor insisting that the other respond just how I want him to.

ARMANDO: You're demanding.

CRYSTAL: I love passion, caresses, humor, lots of kisses, pampering, and getting pampered. No complaints! More kisses, dreaming together, saying I love you, knowing when to shut up, no violence! Sharing time, either one child or two, though three is my favorite number!

ARMANDO: It seems like this cake is half rancid, no?

CRYSTAL: What?

ARMANDO: The cake…try it…it tastes terrible…

CRYSTAL: I can't, I'm on a diet *(writing in her diary, whispering full of irony)* How charming: the guy wants me to try something terrible.

GERRY: And I haven't changed a bit. Except with her it lasted a little longer, 10 years. Imagine that, I spent 10 years with the same woman!

ANNIE: No, I can't imagine…

GERRY: Did you know that a body releases 250 substances when placed before a being whom it finds attractive? It only needs four seconds to form an opinion. Did you know that?

ANNIE: Here they give you seven minutes, presumably to avoid making a mistake.

GERRY: 250 substances. Hormones, acids, gases issued… *(Belching without meaning to)* Pardon me, it must be the coffee, it gives me heartburn… Do you want me to take my glasses off so you can see me better?

ANNIE: You're right, four seconds is more than enough.

The bell rings. Change of couples.

ANNIE: There are many kinds of kisses, and many ways of kissing. There are pecking kisses, where the lips barely meet.

ARMANDO: Right, with puckered lips.

ANNIE: There are marking kisses, violent kisses that come with bites, those that leave their trace in the form of hickeys.

ARMANDO: Hickeys. I'm more the romantic type...

ANNIE: And hot kisses too, with lip nibbles, and subtle licks. Or doggy-style, with the tongue hanging out, drooling on your face, and which tend to come with a juicy passionate fuck.

CRYSTAL: Hypocritical, treacherous kisses, those you don't even feel.

GERRY: And the hypoallergenic ones, that taste of toothpaste, or headaches or sugar free gum.

ARMANDO: Drunken kisses, thanks to a wild night, some pleasant to recall, and others not.

ANNIE: Amnesiac kisses and mental gaps, the fault of memory, or of slow-arriving shame…

ARMANDO and CRYSTAL kiss.
The bell rings.
They wake up next to each other after a drunken night.

CRYSTAL: Me, with that dude? No fucking way! And they took our picture!

ARMANDO: What did you say your name was?

CRYSTAL: Crystal.

ARMANDO: Nice to meet you, Crystal.

The bell rings.
We return to the world of the cafeteria.

CRYSTAL: No need to pray to Cupid for a miracle, because this is a Speed Date.

ARMANDO: All in all there are all sorts of kisses. What are you thinking about?

ANNIE: That there are good kissers, and not. Memorable mouths, and kisses worth remembering…

ARMANDO: And not.

CRYSTAL: My first kiss was so incredible that I can't even remember it…

GERRY: I was fourteen, had gone to the movies with a girl I liked, I knew the kiss was inevitable, believe that both of us were hoping it would happen.

ANNIE: Today I want one of those kisses that soaks your panties, a kiss that gets me hot, and which almost always leads to something more…

CRYSTAL: Those are my favorite…

ARMANDO: Those women were eager to love me.

GERRY looks toward Crystal and Annie.

ARMANDO: No, not them…my mother and my grandmother, they gave up everything, including their own selves, just so I could feel loved. When I was a baby, that love was luxurious, but little by little the luxury turned into a burden, a burden that brought about reproaches, pain, and a whole lot of sacrifices that drove my grandmother to her grave, and my mother to an overwhelming loneliness. In my maternal home I learned that whatever comes, it all ends up empty and forgotten.

ANNIE: Despite his tender age, I had two years on him, rumor was he was a great kisser, so my expectations kept getting more elaborate, more intense…

GERRY: We were at the Belle Epoque Movie Theatre.

ARMANDO: The Belle Epoque! Neither that theatre nor the beauty of that era exist anymore.

GERRY: I don't remember what the movie was but obviously that was the least important thing to me.

CRYSTAL: More popcorn?

Armando chokes on the popcorn, coughs and gags. Annie ends up banging him on the back so that he can get his breath back.

GERRY: Cold, sweaty palms. Soon a glance, saucy eyes, twisted mouth, five, four, three, two…

CRYSTAL: My heart beats faster, I knew that something was about to happen…

ANNIE: Lips that brush, that join, everything is almost perfect…almost, because despite his tender age, the gentleman kisses very well, the only downside is that he drools too much, his saliva is excessive. Gross, I feel like a wet dog. All I want is for it to end. He insists, and I plot my escape.

Crystal launches herself toward a glass of water.

ARMANDO: What's going on!?

CRYSTAL: I spilled my soda. I'll be right back. I'm going to the bathroom!

A mirror game in the bathroom between Annie and Crystal.

ANNIE: My mouth's all red!

CRYSTAL: Like a slut…

ANNIE: I don't like it, I'm not liking this "new experience" that I'm supposed to love.

CRYSTAL: I'm a slut, a slut, a slut…

ANNIE: My first encounter with the world of shared saliva is disgusting.

CRYSTAL: This will be the first of many kisses in the story of my love life.

ANNIE: It tastes bad.

A bell rings. Change of couples.

ARMANDO: At the end of sixth grade I met Marisa, my first girlfriend. We were classmates, with neighboring desks and homes. I liked kissing her. She was two years older than me. We blew kisses to each other in the gardens of our local park. We both entered junior high, and continued dating until our second year there. One Friday night Marisa and I were playing Hide and Seek with some neighbors. While I was concealed in my hiding-place, a neighbor found me to tell me that my girlfriend was kissing other boys, that even he had had the chance to kiss her. He broke my heart in an instant. I went to find

Marisa to tell her what I'd heard. She denied it and left. There I remained, in the door frame of my house, crying. I didn't want to believe her. I preferred drama. I'd claimed my family legacy. After her fifteenth birthday party, Marisa spoke with me, and told me that we couldn't keep going out because she wanted to date an older guy, a 17 year old. A little while later, I asked her little sister to be my girlfriend. She accepted. We didn't last long. It was my revenge on Marisa. One in, one out. It worked. From then on, the kissing bug stayed with me, and I practiced with any girl who'd let me.

A bell rings. Change of couples.

ARMANDO: Is this your first time?

CRYSTAL: What?

ARMANDO: Is this your first time on a speed date?

CRYSTAL: Why? Is it obvious?

GERRY: Some people revel in their own humility. That's not my problem. Where were we?

35

ANNIE *(rotely, out of inertia):* You were telling me about your family…

GERRY: Chapter 11: On how I began beating myself up.

ANNIE: Aha…

GERRY: According to my analyst, those women trained me to love another woman, an extension of them. They…

Noticing Armando looking toward Crystal and Annie.

No, not them…My mother and my grandmother taught me that fidelity rebounds to your credit, that gentlemanliness is repaid with respect and admiration, that a woman doesn't deserve to be hit, or slapped around, even if her mouth has let out the most hurtful of insults, the most cutting slander, the most thoughtless irony.

CRYSTAL: How conscientious of your mother and grandmother. I would have loved to have met them.

GERRY: Whenever you want! They're still alive.

CRYSTAL: Don't make such a fuss...It's just a manner of speaking.

ARMANDO: They raised me to be a sensitive man. And they succeeded! I began falling in love, and I don't say that lightly. Starting at age five, I'd fall in love, suffer, and rend my clothes; love was a fortress to conquer, a continent to populate, a hope: the only one. Until I discovered the true creative and destructive essence of love.

The bells indicate the end of the speed date.
Everyone looks over their notes.

GERRY: Number four, no…number five, even less.

CRYSTAL: How ridiculous with his arrogant swagger, suavely sliding his finger along the edge of his cup…no, there was definitely no chemistry between us.

ANNIE: Number six, no, I don't like divorced guys, they're too crafty.

ARMANDO: Number 3, number 3…what was she like? Right! She was the one who drew imaginary figures on the tablecloth with her index finger, and then crossed her legs to stop me from looking at her thighs…maybe…she has a nice body.

3.3 FRAGMENT/THE CHILD

ARMANDO: What do you want?

ANNIE: I don't know.

ARMANDO: Do you want to keep it?

ANNIE: I don't know. Let's just say that getting pregnant wasn't in my immediate plans. I'm about to start grad school and…truth is I don't know.

ARMANDO: But, do you want us to have it, yes or no?

ANNIE: You don't have a job, and my salary alone isn't enough. I don't think this is the right time.

ARMANDO: The right time for having a child doesn't exist, Anna.

ANNIE: But the reality of it is overwhelming, at least for me.

ARMANDO: Me, I do want it...

ANNIE: ...

ARMANDO: What do you want?

ANNIE: I feel like everything's come to a stop. I don't know which way to go.

ARMANDO: You have doubts, but I believe that we can get through this, entirely whole, and with our child.

ANNIE: For six months, I've been paying all the bills, including the rent. When are you going to make money? You couldn't even manage to look after your family's clock shop. A child is a big responsibility, and I don't want to bear that burden alone.

ARMANDO: I already told you that I'm going to get a job soon, it's not my fault that they let me go from the business and that things are the way they are.

ANNIE: Tell me then: how are things, according to you?

ARMANDO: Fucked.

ANNIE: And yet you want us to have a child. Honestly, I don't understand you.

ARMANDO: It seems like having a child with me would really get in your way.

ANNIE: No. It's just that I have common sense, and I don't want to get stuck in a risky situation.

ARMANDO: What are you saying? A risky situation! That's life.

ANNIE: It's so easy for you to just drift along, since I'm the one who always picks you up when you fall, who always takes responsibility.

ARMANDO: If you're Miss Responsible, why did you let yourself get pregnant?

ANNIE: You're an asshole!

Annie breaks down crying.
Transition.

ARMANDO: I'm sorry. I didn't mean to say that…

ANNIE: What am I going to do?

ARMANDO: What are we going to do? You're not alone in this.

ANNIE: So what are we going to do?

ARMANDO: Solve things.

ANNIE: Lately, I feel like the love that's been solving our problems is the same love that's been fueling them in the first place.

ARMANDO: So then the same love that's led to the problem is the one that will lead us to a solution.

ANNIE: Making a baby is something that you do and at the same that just happens.

ARMANDO: Having a child with you is not in any way a problem for me.

ANNIE: For me having a child feels almost threatening.

ARMANDO: I suggest that we head in a different direction.

ANNIE: Where?

ARMANDO: Toward love, not fear.

6. IN JAKARTA AIRPORT

Gerry and Armando are seated in the boarding area of Jakarta Airport.

ARMANDO: Toward love...

GERRY: What did you say?

ARMANDO: Huh?

GERRY: I didn't quite hear what you said.

ARMANDO: I didn't say anything.

GERRY: Sure, you said something about love.

ARMANDO: Maybe it was a fragment of someone else's conversation.

GERRY: Maybe. Where'd your wife go?

ARMANDO: My wife?

GERRY: Yeah, your wife.

ARMANDO: ...

GERRY: The one who came out of your suitcase just a moment ago.

ARMANDO: Are you feeling all right?

GERRY: I feel fine, I'm not hallucinating, I assure you.

ARMANDO: If you say so, I believe you.

GERRY: Where's your wife?

ARMANDO: I'm traveling alone.

Crystal, the flight attendant, approaches Gerry with affection.

CRYSTAL: I secured you a seat in business class.

GERRY: Excuse me, but I think you're confusing me-

ARMANDO: Playing dumb seems to be working for you.

GERRY: What's the deal with this idiot?

ARMANDO: I'm just writing in my journal.

CRYSTAL: Are you feeling okay, my love? You're sweating.

GERRY: I feel fine but I think you've confused me with someone else.

CRYSTAL: That joke has gone far enough, Gerry.

GERRY: How'd you know my name?

CRYSTAL: I'm your girlfriend. *(To Armando)* Has he been disoriented long?

ARMANDO: I don't know.

CRYSTAL: Sorry, I haven't introduced myself. I'm Crystal Joy.

ARMANDO: Armando Small.

CRYSTAL: Are you waiting for a flight?

ARMANDO: No. I'm investigating the future.

CRYSTAL: What kind of job is that?

ARMANDO: Since the age of twenty I've been keeping a diary of coincidences. Many of them are trivial: people's names that come up unexpectedly in different conversations, airline tickets and coat check tickets with identical numbers, flight times, a sentence out of a book that gets repeated in real life.

CRYSTAL: And what's hiding behind these coincidences?

ARMANDO: A common movement, a common breath.

GERRY: That journal's mine. You took it from me.

ARMANDO: You're wrong, my friend.

CRYSTAL: Gerry, please, calm down.

ARMANDO: All I've been doing is sitting here on this bench for hours taking notes on the people passing by. Here, look.

Armando shows the journal.

ARMANDO: I note their age, their sex, their clothing, and whether they've got suitcases or umbrellas. I also take into account details like the hour, the time of day, the time of year.

GERRY: That's my journal! Give it back!

CRYSTAL: What does it all mean?

ARMANDO: These are the results, I sort them into "Groups of Numbers", very similar to those used by gamblers, statisticians, insurance companies, and polling organizations.

CRYSTAL: Very interesting.

ARMANDO: You know what I call this phenomenon?

CRYSTAL: ...

ARMANDO: The Law of Seriality. Coincidences come in series', which is to say that what gets produced is a repetition in space in which the individual numbers in the sequence aren't connected by the same active cause. This is barely the tip of the iceberg of a much larger cosmic principle.

A light change.

7. DRAWING TIME

Armando draws a clock on Annie's stomach, using her belly button as the center.
We hear the tick tock of a clock.

ANNIE: That tickles.

ARMANDO: Do you know what today is?

ANNIE: Friday.

ARMANDO: And what else?

ANNIE: It's February.

ARMANDO: As of today, we've been together four years.

ANNIE: Really?

ARMANDO: Yes

ANNIE: That was fast!

ARMANDO: Promise me one thing.

ANNIE: What's that?

ARMANDO: Don't die before me.

ANNIE: Armando, why are you talking like that?

ARMANDO: Do you promise?

ANNIE: I promise. What's with you?

ARMANDO: I wish we could freeze time at this instant, forever.

ANNIE: Me too.

ARMANDO: You make me very happy, Anna, did you know that?

ANNIE: Why?

ARMANDO: Because you take me for who I am, with all that implies.

ANNIE: I trust your eyes.

ARMANDO: I already know what we're going to call him.

ANNIE: What?

ARMANDO: Amado.

ANNIE: Amado...I like that.

Armando kisses Annie's stomach. The tick tock of the clock comes to a stop.

8. FLIGHT

Gerry observes in slow motion as Crystal and Armando talk. The atmosphere is rarefied. Gerry speaks but they don't hear him. It's as if he were in a separate reality.

GERRY: A trip to escape myself. Lost bearings. Time without time. Suddenly, a giant moon, nearly half full. It watches like a silent witness. I fly through the air. Thousands of feet above the earth. The ship turns, and the moon hides itself. In the next seat over I read to someone who says "to know pain is to approach wisdom". Small travels. The plane begins its descent, toward solid ground. I like flying, despite vertigo and fears. I lean toward the window. Faint lights make me aware of our arrival in an unknown city. I begin to see it. It's a November night, winter's getting close. The New Year too. These lights are mine. My whole life, illuminated. I breathe deeply, we touch down. Coming home from this trip, I know that I am somehow someone else.

3.4 FRAGMENT/MARRIAGE CONTRACT

Armando and Annie sign the marriage certificate before the Judge, Gerry.

JUDGE: Do you have a marriage contract?

ARMANDO: Yes.

JUDGE: As stipulated in article 76 of the Civil Code, I will read from articles 211 through 214 regarding the rights and responsibilities of spouses. Article 211: Husband and Wife are bound to provide each other with faithfulness, support, and assistance. Article 212: Husband and Wife will together safeguard the moral and material path of the family. They will plan the education and development of their children. Article 213: If the marriage contract doesn't stipulate the proportion of financial contributions, the Husband and Wife will be expected to contribute based upon their respective capabilities. Finally, Article 214: The Husband and Wife are obliged to maintain a life together. Miss Annie Castle, do you accept Mr. Armando Small, here present, as your lawfully wedded husband?

ANNIE: Yes.

JUDGE: Mr. Armando Small, do you accept Miss Annie Castle, here present, as your lawfully wedded wife?

ARMANDO: Yes.

JUDGE: By the power vested in me, I declare you Husband and Wife. Congratulations.

Armando kisses Annie on the lips, and lifts her in the air.

3.5 FRAGMENT/ COINCIDENCE

As Armando is leaving, Annie walks by. They run into each other without meaning to. Lovestruck.

ARMANDO: Excuse me…Annie?

ANNIE: Yes?

ARMANDO: It's me…Armando. Human Resources?

ANNIE: Yes, that's right. How are you, sir?

ARMANDO: What a surprise to see you out of the office, in a bathing suit no less! What are you doing here?

ANNIE: I'm here on vacation.

ARMANDO: When did you arrive? I didn't see you on the plane.

ANNIE: Last night. I missed the charter flight.

ARMANDO: Who'd you come with?

ANNIE: I came alone. My friend, she cancelled on me. And you, sir?

ARMANDO: There's no need to be formal. We're on vacation, right?

ANNIE: And you?

ARMANDO: With Crystal, my partner.

ANNIE: How nice.

ARMANDO: Yes.

ANNIE: ...

ARMANDO: ...

ANNIE: I didn't think it would be so hot...

ARMANDO: Would you like to dine with us?

ANNIE: Okay, sure.

ARMANDO: The hotel restaurant is very good. We'll see you later.

ANNIE: Yes... see you in a bit.

9. GERRY

GERRY: I am an allergic person. I've been like this for as long as I can remember. It's had its challenges. Allergies multiply in me like a plague, and they're constantly mutating, so that what starts out as a light nose tickle, turns into a water faucet draining all the liquid from my body. A frog in the throat becomes a bronchial attack, a tiny little bee sting, slobbering convulsions. Despite all that, I consider myself a healthy person. So long as I'm not having an allergy attack. I've had to put up with all sorts of mutations and complicated evolutions of one allergy into another. I've never had pets since their hair hurts me. Petting a dog, cat, or tiny gerbil would initiate an asthmatic death sentence. Dust keeps me from breathing, pork gives me diarrhea, and chocolate a migraine. Strawberries irritate my skin, and sunlight gives me pre-cancerous spots. But this is nothing compared to the worst of my tragedies, an allergy to saliva. Not my own, of course. I'm allergic to that of others. The contact of human saliva on my delicate skin, or with my own saliva, leads to convulsions, dizziness, acute dermatitis in the armpits, cramps, genital swelling, temporary memory loss, coughing fits, vomiting, hypertension, sinusitis, anxiety attacks, and a pressing need to cry. All this, along with being absolutely inconvenient, has snatched from me one my life's great pleasures: kisses. I can't let anyone kiss me. My personal relationships, or rather, my intimate ones, are limited, and the lack of contact with another mouth, with the saliva of another mouth more precisely, has eroded my love life, which, since this new allergic mutation, is practically nonexistent. My mouth is dry and my heart is slowly but surely falling to pieces.

10. THE KISS BY KLIMT

Crystal and Gerry mimic the postures portrayed in Klimt's "The Kiss". They suddenly start laughing, ever more uncontrollably. They return to kissing in another pictorial position. It's a kind of game. They continue laughing and having fun. They come up with well-known and emblematic words of love.

GERRY *(singing):* You must remember this. A kiss is just a kiss a sigh is just a sigh...

CRYSTAL: Casablanca! My turn:
   Love is a smoke raised with the fume of sighs;
   Being purged, a fire sparkling in lovers' eyes;
   Being vex'd, a sea nourish'd with lovers' tears:

GERRY: Give me a hint.

CRYSTAL: Romeo and...

GERRY: Juliet. William Shakespeare. *He sings* Because your kiss, your kiss is on my list.

CRYSTAL *(singing):* Because your kiss your kiss I can't resist.

Laughter. Transition.

GERRY: I want to read you something that I like very much:
> I never found them again—mine entirely by chance,
> and so easily given up,
> then longed for so painfully.
> The poetic eyes, the pale face,
> those lips—I never found them again.

GERRY: Do you like it?

CRYSTAL: Very much. Who wrote it?

GERRY: Cavafys, one of my favorite poets.
I've looked on beauty so much
that my vision overflows with it.

CRYSTAL: I want to read him.

11. PUBLIC BATHROOM, PRIVATE MIRROR

Mirror scene. Crystal and Annie in the bathroom.

ANNIE: My face is all red.

CRYSTAL: Time is cruel....I'm scared of earthquakes...of the shaking, of collapse.

ANNIE: I saw you...I recognized you...I saw myself in you.

CRYSTAL: Don't confuse similarity with identity. Don't get confused.

ANNIE: Where did you come from?

CRYSTAL: I'm scared of feeling fragile and vulnerable.

ANNIE: Breathe in through the nose, and then breathe out through the nose...

CRYSTAL: Racing heart, panic, my palms are getting sweaty...what am I doing? He has a partner, forget it.

ANNIE: You've asked yourself: How genuine are you, how open and defenseless, how ready are you to feel, to get involved and to expose yourself to yourself, and to everything that concerns you and matters to you.

CRYSTAL: He's your partner's brother. What are you getting me into? I can't! I can't!

ANNIE: Are you ready to face the truth about yourself, or do you prefer to go on believing in your naiveté and innocence, to remain hidden, so deeply withdrawn?

CRYSTAL: That's another one of your questions that I can't answer with a yes or a no!

ANNIE: Breathe in through the nose, and then, breathe out through the nose.

3.6 FRAGMENT: HOLIDAY BY THE SEA

ARMANDO: Annie and I work together. She's in Human Resources.

CRYSTAL: You've never mentioned her.

ARMANDO: Really?

CRYSTAL: Why not?

ARMANDO: I don't know. It's not important. She's just another work colleague, that's all.

CRYSTAL: And so you invited her to eat with us?

ARMANDO: Do you mind?

CRYSTAL: Obviously not. It's just a question.

ARMANDO: She's alone, it seems like her friend cancelled her trip. It's just a little gesture of kindness on my part. Do you mind?

CRYSTAL: It's all the same to me.

ANNIE walks toward Armando and Crystal. She approaches them shyly.

CRYSTAL: Is that Annie?

Armando and Annie wave to each other.

ARMANDO: Yes, that's her.

CRYSTAL: She's pretty...

ANNIE: How's it going?

ARMANDO: This is Crystal.

CRYSTAL: Nice to meet you.

ANNIE: Annie.

ARMANDO: What do you think of the hotel?

ANNIE: Very cute...much better than I'd imagined.

CRYSTAL: Is this your first time in Indonesia?

CAROLINE: Yes, yours?

CRYSTAL: Us too.

ARMANDO: I finally convinced her to take this trip.

CRYSTAL: I would have preferred somewhere closer. Oaxaca, for example. But Armando's got a thing about exotic travel, and so here we are.

ANNIE: It's a beautiful place.

CRYSTAL: The tour is leaving in an hour. I'd like to relax some before we go. If you want, stay here with your friend and we'll meet up later.

ARMANDO: No, I'll come along.

CRYSTAL: Whatever. *(To Annie)* Are you going on the group tour?

ANNIE: I think I'd prefer to sit by the sea for a bit.

CRYSTAL: Okay then, we'll see you later.

ANNIE: Okay, enjoy yourselves.

ARMANDO: What are up to tonight?

ANNIE: I don't know, dancing, I guess, or karaoke.

CRYSTAL: Are you coming?

ARMANDO: Yeah, I'm on my way. Okay, we'll see you later.

12. THE SMALL FAMILY AT THE BEACH

Sounds of the sea.
Puppets of Annie, Armando and their child Amado.
A joyful and happy moment for the Small family at the beach.

ARMANDO/ANNIE *(Calling out into the distance):* Amado!

AMADO: Papa, come into the ocean. Mama, come, mama!

ARMANDO/ANNIE: Waves and waves of love. Waves and waves of love.

13. TWO BEDS FOUR LOVERS

Two couples: Crystal and Armando/Annie and Gerry. Each couple is lying in its respective bed.

GERRY: I'm feeling something here.

CRYSTAL: Where?

ANNIE: Here, look.

CRYSTAL: Here?

ARMANDO: No, there, up.

CRYSTAL: Do you feel it here?

GERRY: No, not so far down! It's more over here.

ANNIE: Here or there?

ARMANDO: There!

CRYSTAL: Here?

GERRY: Yes!

ARMANDO: Ooooh!

GERRY: Do you feel it?

ANNIE: What?

GERRY: Do you feel something?

CRYSTAL: Where?

ARMANDO: Here!

ANNIE: No I don't feel anything.

GERRY: I'm sorry…it's going…

CRYSTAL: What?

ARMANDO: The fear…

GERRY: My fear of falling in love.

ANNIE: Do you love me?

CRYSTAL: Yes…

ARMANDO: How much?

CRYSTAL: A lot.

GERRY: What's a lot?

ANNIE: Too much.

GERRY: In spite of my allergies?

CRYSTAL: Yes, in spite of your allergies.

GERRY: Have I told you the story of my dog, Bear?

CRYSTAL: Yes, a few times….I'm tired. I've taken several flights, and I drank some Crazy Juice too.

GERRY: Crazy Juice?

CRYSTAL: It's a secret potion they make over at Taquito's place.

Crystal sleeps.

ANNIE: You're not sleepy?

GERRY *(writing in his journal):* Same questions, different lovers.

ANNIE: What?

GERRY: Almost not.

ANNIE: Not what?

GERRY: I'm almost not sleepy *(To Annie)* Have I told you the story of how my dog, Bear, got run over?

ANNIE: Bear...It wasn't named Rabbit?

GERRY: Who?

ANNIE: Your dog.

GERRY: My dog was named Bear.

ANNIE: Your dog reminds me of a friend I have whom we call Cat.

GERRY: Is she the one who has a cat named Cow?

ANNIE: Yes, her! Mmm. I'm sleepy.

GERRY: So, I've already told you the story of how my dog, Bear, got run over?

ANNIE: Your little dog…Bear…Mmm. I'm sleepy.

GERRY: I was coming home from school. I was seven or eight. Suddenly, as I approached the corner of our street, my brother rode toward me on his bike. As soon as he got to me he said: "I've got some bad news. Your dog got run over".

ANNIE: Poor thing…Poor Bear…

GERRY: Obviously I didn't believe him, for me death simply didn't exist. I couldn't imagine what this dying thing even was. But my brother insisted: "Come on so you can see that it's true".

CRYSTAL: Poor thing…Poor Bear…

GERRY: And off we go, running up the street. A little ways away, about even with our garage, I spot a dark lump lying in the middle of the street. Something began to happen in my body. I was overcome with a burst of adrenaline that left me speechless and in a cold sweat. I ran, ran, and ran without stopping. Lying on the pavement, immobile, with a smashed head, was my Bear. My friend whom I'd played with. I'd seen him just that morning.

ANNIE: Go to sleep already.

CRYSTAL: ... *(snores lightly)*

GERRY: I loved lying around with him, rolling on the floor in the afternoons when I got home from school. He made me giggle when he chewed on my ear. How I played with that dog. How I loved him. Bear revealed Death's power to me. I ran screaming until I was inside my house. I threw myself onto the floor crying and raging for my dog. My Bear, My Bear! I was certain that I'd never get to play with him again. My world collapsed the moment I saw him lying on the pavement, lifeless. My life cracked in a second. My dad wrapped him in newspapers, and put him in a bag. We buried Bear in the field behind our house. We walked all the way there that day to say goodbye to my friend. Bear, the first death in my life.

ARMANDO: Why are you telling them all this?

GERRY: I haven't felt like that since Bear the dog got run over...so alone.

Gerry sleeps. Armando tosses and turns, groaning in a dream. Annie wakes up.

ANNIE: Why do I never feel whole, full, complete? I want something that I don't have, and when I get the thing that I wanted yesterday, soon enough it no longer matters to me because I always want something more. More kisses, more caresses, to make love, to kiss you....but you don't want to. I'm never quite satisfied. If we could only live without wanting anything....these days I just want to add more names to my ledger of love. I'm curious. The smell of a man stays on your skin for at least two or three days, his breath too. Nothing else smells like him.

Annie sleeps, groaning in a dream.

CRYSTAL: There are days when patience and love fade away. I start to find you repulsive. I'm irritated by the most basic everyday things: how you leave the towel on the bed, how you dance, how you eat. Just thinking that you want to kiss or touch me makes me nauseous. There have been times when I've had sex without enjoying it, out of habit. I've felt empty, hoping only that you might finish soon so that I could get on with other things. I've felt used, undesirable, unappreciated. Why do I allow myself to feel that way? Dreams help us to know ourselves better. It's time to wake up.

The two couples return to their initial positions in bed. They wake up.

3.7 FRAGMENT/WAKING UP

ANNIE: Have you been up long?

ARMANDO: A little while.

ANNIE: What's the world got to say for itself?

ARMANDO: The same old shit: crises, wars and hate.

ANNIE: Your indignation about the state of humanity gets you even crankier than waking up early.

ARMANDO: ...

ANNIE: If it ruins your mood to read the paper, why do you do it?

ARMANDO: Out of habit, like so many other things.

ANNIE: For example?

ARMANDO: Fucking.

ANNIE: ...

ARMANDO: Don't give me that look. You asked, I answered.

ANNIE: I slept badly last night. I had nightmares.

ARMANDO: What a coincidence.

ANNIE: I dreamed that I entered a house looking for a man whom I used to really like a long time ago, and along the way I came across two other men, friends of his.

ARMANDO: And then what? Did you have a ménage a trois?

ANNIE: Believe it or not, it didn't go like that.

ARMANDO: ...

ANNIE: Along the way, I stopped and watched those two men.

ARMANDO: Were they twins?

ANNIE: No, they weren't twins. Would you stop interrupting?

ARMANDO: ...

ANNIE: I asked those two men...

ARMANDO: Who weren't twins...

ANNIE: Where is my love?

ARMANDO: Can you pass the sugar?

ANNIE: They replied: taking a shower. I remember that I tried the shower door, but it was locked and wouldn't open. Then the two men helped me and opened it for me. He was nude, and wet. Top to bottom. I approached him and said, "I want to tell you something." Then he took my hands and we stared into each other's eyes. Suddenly we both spoke at the same time: "I like you". And we kissed.

ARMANDO: Why are you telling me this?

ANNIE: Do you mind?

ARMANDO: I hate it when you start talking just to try and seduce me.

ANNIE: What are you saying?

ARMANDO: I'm going to take a shower.

ANNIE: Why don't we ever make love?

ARMANDO: We made love last night.

ANNIE: Yeah, I know, for the first time in three months...but...

ARMANDO: What?

ANNIE: Forget it...

ARMANDO: Nothing is enough for you.

ANNIE: No, it's not that.

ARMANDO: Then, what is it?

ANNIE: Why the hell don't you touch me anymore? Why do you avoid me, and give me absurd excuses, so that I have to scream and beg for you to touch me!?

ARMANDO: I'm going to take a shower.

ANNIE: You're rejecting me.

ARMANDO: ...

ANNIE: For months now you've been very distant with me. Why?

ARMANDO: It is way too early in the morning to start an argument.

ANNIE: I don't want to argue...I want us to talk. I feel empty, incomplete.

ARMANDO: ...

ANNIE: Say something.

ARMANDO: What do you want me to say?

ANNIE: I don't know, something, anything.

ARMANDO: I think you're only concerned with yourself and your own measly individual happiness, and that's why you don't feel complete.

ANNIE: Your words are a wound that won't close.

ARMANDO: You wanted us to talk, right?

ANNIE: Whose words were daggers?

ARMANDO: Who felt the stab?

ANNIE: I'm going to take a shower.

14. THE EMBRACE

Airport.
Gerry waits for Crystal's flight after not having seen her in a while. He searches for her among the crowd.
Armando accompanies Annie to see her off. They're carrying Amado, who's an infant.

GERRY: Cryssy! Crystal! I'm over here!

CRYSTAL: My love!

Gerry and Crystal push through the crowd until they find each other, and join together in a loving embrace.

GERRY: You look amazing!

CRYSTAL: I missed you so much...

GERRY: You smell so good.

CRYSTAL: I love you I love you I love you.

Armando sees Annie and the baby off.

ARMANDO: You behave Amado and give my best to your grandmother. Call me as soon as you get there.

ANNIE: Yes.

ARMANDO: You got everything: the feeding bottles, the diapers, those drops the pediatrician prescribed?

ANNIE: Don't worry. I've got it all here.

ARMANDO: I wish I could've come with you, seriously.

ANNIE: It's fine. Besides one of us has got to work. We'll be fine.

ARMANDO: Please give my best to your mom.

ANNIE: I left you some steamed veggies in the fridge. Pasta too.

ARMANDO: I'm going to miss you both a lot. Take care.

ANNIE: We'll miss you too.

15. THE INTENSITY OF ALTITUDE

Crystal, dressed in her flight attendant's uniform.

CRYSTAL: Today I've decided to come out of the closet. Today I feel happy and whole because I've managed to accept myself for who I am. For a long time I was keeping this secret which was tormenting me and keeping me from being free, but now I've decided to live with my new condition. I am...a closet intensive. Well I was a closet intensive, but now I'm simply intense. But my passion for me remains whole. I used to suffer for love, I didn't understand why men were removing themselves from my life.

They'd flee terrified after a few weeks, or sometimes hours. Now I understand, my intensity drove them away. My way of living love down to the marrow, of taking it as far as it could go, to the point of ripping out my soul and loving them crushingly and suffocatingly...they'd get nervous and flee in terror. Now that I know the cause, I need only to wait for the right man. I have faith that this man exists, and will appear one day. Meanwhile, I'm living my life, and hoping that love will surprise me. *(she begins to break down)*. I'm happy, I feel great, I'm very okay, I'm feeling totally awesome... *(she starts crying)*

Transition. The flight attendant pushes her cart. Meanwhile she sings the song of "The Intense Suicides." Armando and Annie make love in the plane's bathroom.

VOICE *(Off)*: Our captain has begun the initial descent. Please fasten your seatbelts, and in few brief minutes we will be landing in Mexico City.

CRYSTAL:
I want to rip out my eyes and kill myself.
I want to do myself in 'cause you can't love me.
Oh yes, oh yes!
I want to die, to die, to die, to die
want to die, to die, to die, to die

want to throw myself down a well and drown myself.
want to cut my veins until the blood runs dry.
Oh yes, oh yes!
I want to die, to die, to die, to die
want to die, to die, to die, to die
I don't want to be alone, I'd prefer a lousy lover
I'd rather be dead than feel no love from another
Oh yes, oh yes!
I want to die, to die, to die, to die
Oh yes I want to die to die to die to die
I prefer death to living without you.

Orgasm in the plane restroom. Armando and Annie return to their seats.

CRYSTAL: I used to be like that, intensely negative, now I'm just intensely joyful. Before, I thought about death, about slitting my wrists, about putting my head in the oven, in honor of Sylvia Plath, and suffocating myself with gas. Of throwing myself from an overpass smack into the middle of the highway and forgetting my miserable life. I used to get depressed, and stay in my room for days at a time. I suffered intensely for love. Now no. I'm really fine, and I'm so, but so, happy, I've come to accept my intensity, and I'm glad to be living to love's limit.

16. LOUD LOVE

CRYSTAL and GERRY make love at full volume.

CRYSTAL: Don't stop, don't stop! Ohhhh I'm flying!

GERRY: Higher, higher, higher...

CRYSTAL: Yes, higher, higher! Yes, yes, yes!

GERRY: That's it, that's it, that's it, that's it...

CRYSTAL: Woooooaaaaaa....

GERRY: Ahhhhhh!

CRYSTAL: That was incredible! I loved it!

GERRY: Isn't it amazing how you and I fit together perfectly? Your hands fit in mine: you're the bird and I'm the nest. Your breasts mold to my chest, and your ass to my stomach. My legs are embracing yours, and my arms too.

CRYSTAL: You're an octopus in love with my sponge.

GERRY: Even our bellies belong together. Just look at it! I adore your body in mine.

CRYSTAL: It's the first time that your skin hasn't been irritated after making love.

GERRY: I'm floating in a paradise of orgasms.

3.8 FRAGMENT/THE BETRAYAL

Two couples: Armando and Annie/Crystal and Gerry. Armando and Crystal chop an onion with a knife. Annie and Gerry arrive.

ANNIE *(to Armando):* What are you making?

GERRY *(to Crystal):* What are you making?

ARMANDO: An omelet.

CRYSTAL: An omelet.

ANNIE: What time did you get in last night?

GERRY: What time did you get in last night?

CRYSTAL: I don't know, late.

ARMANDO: I don't know, late.

ANNIE: I came by to get you. I was knocking on the door, but no one would open it for me.

GERRY: I came by to get you. I was knocking on the door, but no one would open it for me.

CRYSTAL: ...

ARMANDO: ...

ANNIE: Will you look at me?

GERRY: Will you look at me?

CRYSTAL: ...

ARMANDO: ...

ANNIE: You like her a lot, don't you?

GERRY: You like him a lot, don't you?

CRYSTAL: Don't you fucking interrogate me.

ARMANDO: Don't you fucking interrogate me.

ANNIE: Did you fuck her?

GERRY: Did you fuck him?

CRYSTAL: ...

ARMANDO: ...

ANNIE: I knew it!

GERRY: I knew it!

CRYSTAL: Can I tell you why?

ARMANDO: Can I tell you why?

ANNIE: What for! What possible justification could you have for fucking your brother's girlfriend?

GERRY: What for! What possible justification could you have for fucking my brother?

CRYSTAL: I've had it up to here with your jealousy, with your controlling ways.

ARMANDO: I've had it up to here with your jealousy, with your controlling ways.

ANNIE: And me like a fool, up all night, worried about you, thinking something could've happened, that maybe you'd been in an accident...

GERRY: And me like a fool, up all night, worried about you, thinking something could've happened, that maybe you'd been in an accident...

CRYSTAL: My apologies.

ARMANDO: My apologies.

ANNIE: I was very worried about you.

GERRY: I was very worried about you.

CRYSTAL: Really, I'm sorry.

ARMANDO: Really, I'm sorry.

ANNIE: Why would you do this to me? You know I love you.

GERRY: Why would you do this to me? You know I love you.

CRYSTAL: I can't stand the tyranny of your kindness.

ARMANDO: I can't stand the tyranny of your kindness.

ANNIE: I think only of you.

GERRY: I think only of you.

CRYSTAL: I'm not your daughter.

ARMANDO: I'm not your son.

ANNIE: You're acting like you are.

GERRY: You're acting like you are.

CRYSTAL: If you crowd me too much, you'll get what's coming to you.

ARMANDO: If you crowd me too much, you'll get what's coming to you.

ANNIE: Do you need to fuck someone else to get your twisted dose of love?

GERRY: Do you need to fuck someone else to get your twisted dose of love?

CRYSTAL: Shut up already!

ARMANDO: Shut up already!

ANNIE: You're a bastard!

GERRY: You're a bitch!

CRYSTAL: Leave me alone.

ARMANDO: Leave me alone.

ANNIE: We kill what we love.

GERRY: We kill what we love.

CRYSTAL: You're pathetically arrogant. This is the height of your patheticness!

ARMANDO: You're pathetically arrogant. This is the height of your patheticness!

ANNIE: Go to hell!

GERRY: Go to hell!

Physical violence.

ARMANDO: No, you go to hell!

CRYSTAL: Don't scream at me!

ANNIE: Don't touch me!

GERRY: I'll scream if I want to scream!

ARMANDO: Who do you think you are to send me to hell?

ANNIE: What's your deal?

GERRY: How long have you been fucking my brother?

ARMANDO: You've been sending everything to hell for a long time!

ANNIE: What are you talking about? Let me go, you're hurting me!

CRYSTAL: I fell in love without meaning to!

GERRY: Do you think I'm such an idiot that I'd swallow that shit?

ARMANDO: Don't play dumb Annie: you know exactly what I'm talking about!

ANNIE: No, I don't know. All I know is that you're the asshole who's been fucking his brother's little girlfriend. You disgust me.

CRYSTAL: I'll fuck whomever I want! Who are you to stop me?

GERRY: Little fucking bitch!

CRYSTAL: Nasty little allergic. Everything hurts you, even making love!

ARMANDO: I disgust you so much that you preferred to abort instead of doing what we'd agreed!

ANNIE: And you think it was easy for me? Is that what you think!?

ARMANDO You lied to me, and in the end you did whatever you wanted!

ANNIE: I couldn't do it, not at that moment!

GERRY: You're full of lies, of cheap tricks!

CRYSTAL: And you're full of allergies that keep you from loving me! I can't touch you without making you sick!

ARMANDO: Why is it that you're always right about everything in this relationship and I have to keep swallowing garbage and giving in, giving in, always giving in.

GERRY: Armando and you disgust me!

CRYSTAL: Don't you raise your fist at me again. Do you hear me?

Crystal smacks Gerry.

ANNIE: We had Amado, isn't that enough for you?

ARMANDO: I love my son, but before that, you aborted me and mine.

GERRY: He doesn't love you as much.

Annie and Crystal on a second level
Gerry and Armando dispute in front.

ARMANDO: How could you know that?

GERRY: 'Cause it's the truth. You only think about yourself.

ARMANDO: I understand you're angry, but what can you do, these things happens.

GERRY: Cynical shit, you have no idea what loyalty is.

ARMANDO: How do you expect a woman to love you if you can't fuck because you'll break out in hives.

Violent brawl between the brothers.
The two couples separate.
A change of time.

17. THE BAGGAGE

The four characters pack their suitcases.

GERRY: I'm taking our kisses, our beautiful bodies joined together.

CRYSTAL: I'm taking your smile. The first day that we laughed together.

ARMANDO: I'm taking your smell. Your face between my hands.

ANNIE: I'm taking my fear of abandonment. The tears I've borne since childhood.

GERRY: I'm taking your lies. My disappointment.

CRYSTAL: I'm taking the guilt, and your accusations.

ARMANDO: I'm taking the son we didn't have.

ANNIE: I'm taking all the flowers that you gave me.

GERRY: I'm taking your breath. The sound of the key turning when you opened the door.

CRYSTAL: I'm taking your tickles and my hopes of travelling with you.

ARMANDO: I'm taking your pain. Your endless discontent.

ANNIE: I'm taking your fear. Your rancor.

GERRY: I'm taking my pleasure.

CRYSTAL: I'm taking your plans for a future with me.

ARMANDO: I'm taking your criticisms. Your moral superiority.

ANNIE: I'm taking your jealousy. Your lack of understanding.

GERRY: I'm taking your secrets. The books that we read together.

CRYSTAL: I'm taking my hopes of always going to the same place.

ARMANDO: I'm taking everything that we put in, and that we didn't have the courage to give to each other.

ANNIE: I'm taking our attempts to resolve the irresolvable.

GERRY: I'm taking my camera. The photos of us together.

CRYSTAL: I'm taking the frying-pan you learned to cook with.

ARMANDO: I'm taking my sadness. All of my dirty clothes.

ANNIE: I'm taking my orgasms.

GERRY: I'm taking all of my expectations.

CRYSTAL: I'm taking my lovers.

ARMANDO: I'm taking my music collection.

GERRY: I'm taking your love. Waves and waves of love.

CRYSTAL: I'm taking your love. Waves and waves of love.

ARMANDO: I'm taking your love. Waves and waves of love.

ANNIE: I'm taking your love. Waves and waves of love.

ARMANDO: How does a man look at a woman whom he has lost?

ANNIE: How does a woman look at a man who's leaving?

GERRY: How do they look at God?

CRYSTAL: And how does God, supposing that He exists, look at them?

Transition.
Gerry closes the suitcase.
The lovers head in different directions.
They each head their own way.

18. PALM LINES

Image: A couple walking while holding hands. They switch to take the hand of another person. Annie, always the same, goes to change couples to take the hands of Gerry and Armando. Until finally she avoids taking anyone's hand.
Annie comes to a stop alone in front of her reflection, Crystal.

ANNIE: Someone said: you can't leave.

CRYSTAL: And I left.

ANNIE: I told him: stay.

CRYSTAL: And he left.

ANNIE: I don't feel anything.

CRYSTAL: I'm anaesthetized.

ANNIE: I look at my life as if I were seeing it through a dirty, steamed-up window.

CRYSTAL: I'm tired.

ANNIE: A son is no substitute for a partner. I can't be in love with my child.

CRYSTAL: I'm a bad mother.

ANNIE: Unhappiness is easy.

CRYSTAL: Did I tell you my technique for dealing with unhappiness? It's simple.

ANNIE: Close your eyes. Now hold onto the images of people who aren't here. Ready.

CRYSTAL: Deep love gets inside us. That's why it hurts.

ANNIE: Feeling pain is hard. I can't move.

CRYSTAL: You go around in circles. You relive moments from the past, and you can't free yourself. Reproach and accusation. Reproach and accusation.

ANNIE: Most feelings are bullshit, which means they aren't real.

CRYSTAL: I exalt in my pain.

ANNIE: And you carry it with you like a piece of scenery.

ANNIE/CRYSTAL: It's awful.

19. THE GOODBYE

ARMANDO *(to Annie):* The appointment is at the courthouse, at eight am.

ANNIE: Are you sure this is what you want?

ARMANDO: We have passed beyond even the deepest of humiliations. I'm sure.

ANNIE: I feel guilty.

ARMANDO: We have the courage to bear this guilt.

ANNIE: My stomach hurts.

ARMANDO: So I'll see you next Monday?

ANNIE: Yes, at eight, right?

ARMANDO: Yes. At eight.

ANNIE: Are you and Crystal still together?

ARMANDO: Yes...

ANNIE: Sorry. I don't want to know anything. Better you don't tell me.

ARMANDO: It's fine.

ANNIE: What we're doing is for the best. Right?

ARMANDO: Yes.

ANNIE: If you go, that's it. Don't come looking for me.

ARMANDO: Don't worry, I won't.

ANNIE: Leave the house keys on the table.

ARMANDO: Goodbye Annie.

ANNIE: Goodbye.

20. EPILOGUE

CRYSTAL: Why did you get divorced?
ARMANDO: Because I fell in love with my brother's woman.

CRYSTAL: No, seriously.

ARMANDO: Because I fell in love with you.

CRYSTAL: The first time I saw you, you acted like a fool.

ARMANDO: It made me jealous to see you with my brother.

CRYSTAL: Why did you divorce Annie?

ARMANDO: Maybe 'cause of a lack of commitment.

CRYSTAL: But you were together for over ten years.

ARMANDO: And so?

CRYSTAL: Ten years is a long time.

ARMANDO: The lack of commitment doesn't change with time. It was there from the beginning and we never knew how to work it out.

CRYSTAL: But the ties between you and Annie were strong.

ARMANDO: The ties that bind us to others aren't always easy to explain or comprehend.

ANNIE: We had a son.

CRYSTAL *(to Annie):* You must hate me.

ANNIE: I still feel betrayed.

GERRY: Why my brother?

CRYSTAL: I don't know. It just happened.

ANNIE: What does that even mean?

ARMANDO: Do you think it's easy to answer your question?

GERRY: Do you think it's easy to accept your betrayal?

CRYSTAL: Do you think it's easy to bear the guilt?

ANNIE: Do you think it's easy to see things for what they are?

Armando and Crystal kiss passionately.
Gerry and Annie watch the kiss.
They take their suitcases and go.

3.9 FINAL FRAGMENT

GERRY: How did your wife die?

ARMANDO: Ex-wife. We'd been divorced two years.

GERRY: ...

ARMANDO: She was in a crash on the highway.

GERRY: When we recall the recent events of our life, we can easily see the choices we should have made.

ARMANDO: She was on her way to the country house that her current partner and her had just bought.

GERRY: What prevents us from making those decisions when they're right in front of us?

ARMANDO: She drove off the road, and smashed into a tree. They both died instantly.

GERRY: I'm truly sorry to hear it.

ARMANDO: Love contains something unpredictable and unknown. When I met her I never imagined that our story would end the way it did.

GERRY: Why are you taking this trip?

ARMANDO: One thinks that one is a man and that one has worked hard and that now one might allow oneself something good. So this man leaves his house to travel abroad.

GERRY: And suddenly he arrives at an airport that has a sign with enormous letters that reads "Theatre of the World".

ARMANDO: The man thinks, this is the right place. And he buys an airline ticket.

GERRY: Then he sits down in the boarding area and waits. Soon the lights come down, and the performance begins.

ARMANDO: The man realizes: I know this play, it's nothing new to me.

GERRY: And as he is watching, he discovers that this is it, the play that he himself is performing.

ARMANDO: Where did you and I meet?

GERRY: In multiple dimensions: at this moment we can choose whichever one you want.

21. LIFE TRIP

An airport. Two men in the boarding area. Each man drags a rolling suitcase. They sit down beside each other.

ARMANDO: "There are only two kinds of thoughts: memories and imagination."

GERRY: I was alone. It was night. The plane had been delayed for more than three hours. But, what are three hours on eternity's clock?

ARMANDO: Looks interesting...

GERRY: ...

ARMANDO: The book.

GERRY: It's not a book.

ARMANDO: Are you travelling alone?

GERRY: Yes. And you?

ARMANDO: No. I'm travelling with my wife.

Armando opens his suitcase and removes an urn.

GERRY: Where are you taking her?

ARMANDO: To the sea.

GERRY: A nice place to say goodbye.

ARMANDO: I loved this woman very much.

GERRY: I know.

ARMANDO: How do you know?

GERRY: All relationships have an invisible soul: I too have loved a woman.

ARMANDO: Are we talking about the same person?

GERRY: We're talking about love.

ARMANDO: But are we talking about the same thing?

Distant music.

GERRY: ...Do you hear the music?

ARMANDO: It's an orchestra.

GERRY: The orchestra tunes its instruments to hear the music of future nostalgia.

ARMANDO: It's a lovely sound.

GERRY: Stay with the music. If you stay with any emotion long enough, you will discover how it ends in silence.

END